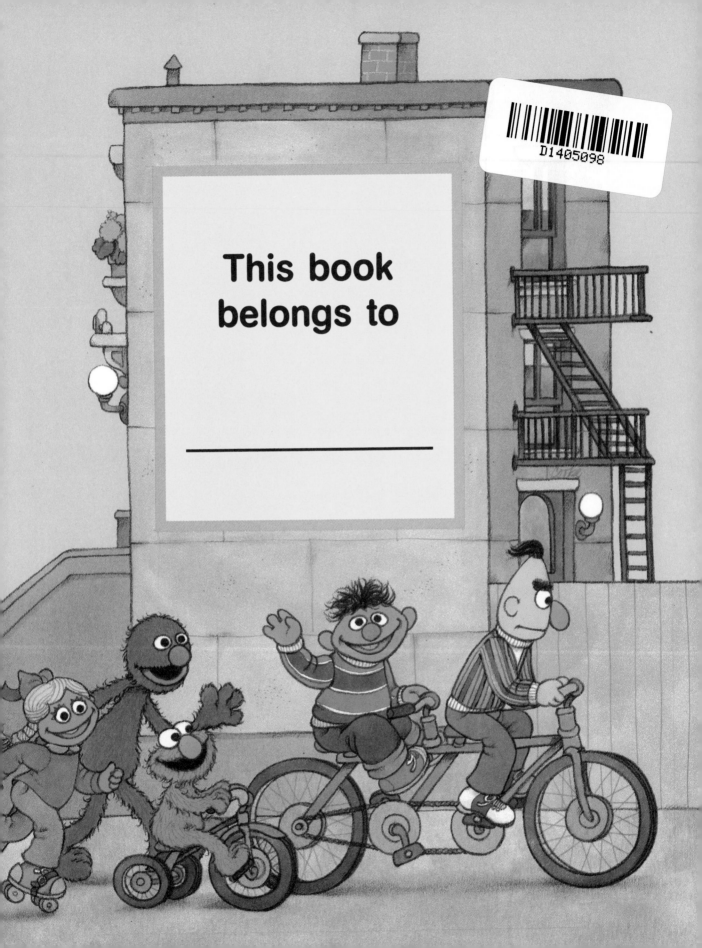

This book
belongs to

_____

ON MY WAY WITH SESAME STREET

Volume 8

My Family

Featuring Jim Henson's Sesame Street Muppets

Children's Television Workshop/Funk & Wagnalls

Authors

Linda Hayward
Jeffrey Moss
Michaela Muntean
Rae Paige
Emily Thompson
Pat Tornborg

Illustrators

Tom Cooke
Robert Dennis
Tom Leigh
Kimberly A. McSparran
Carol Nicklaus
Anne Sikorski
Maggie Swanson
Richard Walz
Jean Zallinger

0-8343-0082-6   1 2 3 4 5 6 7 8 9 0

A Parents' Guide to MY FAMILY

This book reinforces the concept of family. It introduces children to members of the family from Baby Monster to Granny Bird. Children will also learn about different kinds of families and some of the things they do together.

"Baby Monsters" is a story about what baby monsters must know to become big monsters. They learn to comb their fur, make scary faces, and to mind their monster manners!

"If I Lived Alone" is a realistic look at family life. Sometimes it's annoying to share a room with your big sister, but it's nice to have someone to huddle with during a thunderstorm. Sometimes it's annoying to be quiet while the baby naps, but it's nice to have someone who shares his crackers with you.

Some of the activities in this book encourage children to talk about their own families. "Bedtime Stories," "Sweet Dreams," and "Daddy Monster Cooks Dinner" are about family routines that help children feel secure.

We hope that some of these stories remind your children of your own family, and that others teach them about different families.

The Editors
SESAME STREET BOOKS

Baby Monsters

Baby monsters are just like other babies. They need lots of love and care.

Monster mommies sing monster lullabies to their babies. Monster daddies take their babies for walks in the park.

Baby monsters have many
things to learn before they
become grown-up monsters.

Little monsters must learn
to keep their fur neat and tidy.

"Remember to comb your
elbows and behind your
knees," daddy monsters
say.

Some monsters like to look scary, so they go to
scary-face classes. Today the teacher is showing
the little monsters how to make a monster frown.

"Be careful not to scare yourselves," the monster
teacher reminds them.

No matter how big or strong or furry or scary-looking little monsters grow up to be, they always remember their monster manners.

"Excuse me, sir," Herry says every time he bumps into someone.

And little monsters never forget to give monster-size hugs to the monsters they love.

Farley's Family Album

SPOT

GRANDMA and GRANDPA JONES

AUNT SHARON and UNCLE HENRY

Momm

COUSIN PETER

BROTHER FREDDIE

ME (FARLEY)

GRANDMOTHER and GRANDFATHER Smith

ROLLO

nD DADDY

AUNT BESSIE and UNCLE JOHN

SISTER BETSY

COUSIN HENRIETTA

COUSIN HORTENSE

If I Lived Alone

This is where I live.

My Mommy and Daddy live here.
My big sister Frieda and little
brother Roger live here.

Sometimes it's noisy in my house.

Sometimes it's crowded in my house.

Sometimes I have to be quiet because Roger is asleep.

Sometimes I wish I lived alone.

I could have a room all to myself, and I could sit quietly all by myself or make as much noise as I wanted.

But if I lived alone, I wouldn't have anyone to talk to when it rains and thunders.

If I lived alone, I could eat chocolate ice cream for breakfast, vanilla ice cream for lunch, and strawberry ice cream for dinner. And I could eat as much as I wanted.

But if I lived alone, I wouldn't get to have any of Daddy's super-duper, flip-flop flapjacks.

If I lived alone, I wouldn't have to share my toys and books.

But if I lived alone, who would read to me?

If I lived alone, I could stay up as late as I wanted to.

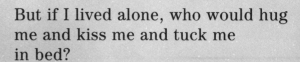
But if I lived alone, who would hug me and kiss me and tuck me in bed?

If I lived alone, I wouldn't have to help set the table, or pick up my toys, or do anything I didn't want to do.

But if I lived alone, who would put a bandage on my knee if I fell down?

If I lived alone, who would play baseball with Daddy?

Who would help him weed the garden?

If I lived alone, who would help Mommy with her sculpture?

Who would talk to her when she takes Roger for a walk?

If I lived alone, who would listen to Frieda's secrets?

Who would share Roger's crackers?

I guess I can't live alone — because if I lived alone, *everyone* would be lonely.

How Do Parents Carry Their Babies?

Parents carry their babies around in many different ways.

A baby kangaroo lives in its mother's pouch for about six months.

A monkey parent can swing through the trees with a baby monkey hanging onto its neck.

A beaver parent sometimes carries its baby cradled in its arms.

Young opossums
hold on to their mother's
fur as she walks.

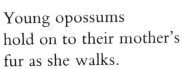

A father seahorse carries
seahorse eggs in a pouch
until the eggs hatch.

Human babies sometimes ride
on their parents' backs.

A mother cat
sometimes carries her kitten
by the scruff of the neck.

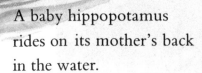

A baby hippopotamus
rides on its mother's back
in the water.

People in My Family

I've got five people in my family, and those five people make me glad.

There's a sister and two brothers.

And a mother and a dad.

Five is such a pretty number. I'm awfully glad that I've
Five people in my family. **1 2 3 4 5**

I've got five monsters in my family, and we all have lots of fun.

Furry wife and scary husband.

Fuzzy daughters, hairy son.

Five is such a scary number. Oh, I'm so glad that I've
Five monsters in my family. **1 2 3 4 5**

I've got five fingers on my left hand, I've got five fingers on my right.
Five fingers help me wave good morning, help me brush my teeth at night.

Five is such a pretty number. I'm awfully glad that I've
Five fingers on each hand. **1   2   3   4   5**

Oh, five is such a pretty number. I'm awfully glad that I've
Five people in my family.

A LA PEANUT BUTTER SOUP!

A La Peanut Butter Soup!

To serve four—

What you need:

1 cup of milk

1 can, or 1½ cups of chicken broth

3 tablespoons of chunky peanut butter

½ teaspoon of onion flakes

¼ teaspoon each of salt and paprika

Note: Adult supervision is suggested.

What you do:

Put some water in the bottom half of a double boiler, and put all your ingredients in the top half (not the top hat). Put the double boiler over medium heat. Stir the soup until the peanut butter melts and everything is blended together. The peanut chunks will float on top. When the soup comes to a boil, turn the heat very low and simmer it for 10 minutes.

At Home with Slimey

Slimey has his own little house under the ground
where he likes to sleep and eat and watch TV.
Help Slimey get to his house.
Use your finger to trace his path.

A Quilt for Big Bird

Granny Bird made a quilt for Big Bird.
She made it out of patches.

On each patch she sewed a letter.
Some of the letters are P's — for Patch.
Some of the letters are Q's — for Quilt.

Point to the P's.
Point to the Q's.

Dear Granny Bird,
  Thank you for my nice new
quilt. I am learning my P's
and Q's.

      Love,
      Big Bird

Hugs and Kisses

Dear Granny Bird,
I love you.
Big Bird
X X X X X O O
O O O O

Can you find the X's and O's at the bottom of Big Bird's letter?
The X's are for kisses.
The O's are for hugs.
Big Bird is sending lots of hugs and kisses to Granny Bird.

Dear Big Bird,
I love you too.
Granny Bird
X X X X
O O O O

Granny Bird sent some
hugs and kisses to Big Bird too.

Daddy Monster Cooks Dinner

Daddy Monster is making dinner for Baby Monster. What do you like to eat for dinner?

Grover Takes Care of Baby

While walking home from the playground one day Grover dropped his ball, and it rolled right under a baby carriage.

"Please excuse me," said Grover. "Oh, hello, Marsha! Who is this?"

"Hi, Grover," said Marsha. "This is Max, my baby brother. I'm taking care of him while Mommy and Daddy are at work."

"Oh, he is cute and adorable!" said Grover. "What do you do with him?"

"I play with him, take him for walks, help feed him, give him his baths, and put him to bed," said Marsha.

"I would like to take care of a baby, too," said Grover. "I have a new baby cousin named Emily. I, lovable, helpful old Grover, would take good care of the baby Emily."

Grover waved good-bye to Marsha and Max.

I would let Emily play with my toys. I would show her how to climb mountains. . .

go through tunnels. . .

and leap tall buildings in a single bound!

If baby Emily came for a visit,
she could take a nap in my zoo.

I would help get her dressed.

I would introduce Emily to all my friends at play group. Oh, I would be so proud!

But what if she tore my picture? Oh, I would be so embarrassed!

Mrs. Brown would say, "Never mind, Grover, we can fix it."

After play group, we could go shopping. . .

and for a walk.

We could do our exercises together. One and two and — pant, pant! — three. Now touch those toes!

We could play peekaboo . . .

and eensy-weensy spider.

At dinnertime I would help my mommy feed
Emily in her high chair. I would tie on her bib, and
make sure her milk wasn't too hot, and cut up her
carrots, and wipe up her dribbles.

At bathtime I would be ready.

I would pour in the bubbles and test the temperature.

Then I would duck.

At bedtime I would help Emily
listen to a story.

Then I would sing her a lullaby, kiss her nose, and turn on the
night-light. I would even let her borrow my teddy monster to cuddle.

"Good night, Baby Emily."

"I, Grover, would be a big help," he said proudly.

"Oh, Grover, I am so glad you are home," said Grover's mommy as she opened the door of their apartment. "Guess what! Aunt Betsy and Uncle Ralph are bringing your baby cousin, Emily, for a visit. How would you like to help take care of the baby?"

So when Emily came, Grover fed her in the high chair. He tied on her bib, made sure her milk wasn't too hot, cut up her carrots, and wiped her dribbles.

"Grover, you are very good at taking care of baby monster!" said his mommy.

Family Pet

Baby Monster is petting the kitty. Do you have any pets in your family? What pet would you like to have?

Bedtime Stories

Daddy Monster is reading a bedtime story to Baby Monster. What is your favorite bedtime story?

MONSTER GOOSE

Sweet Dreams

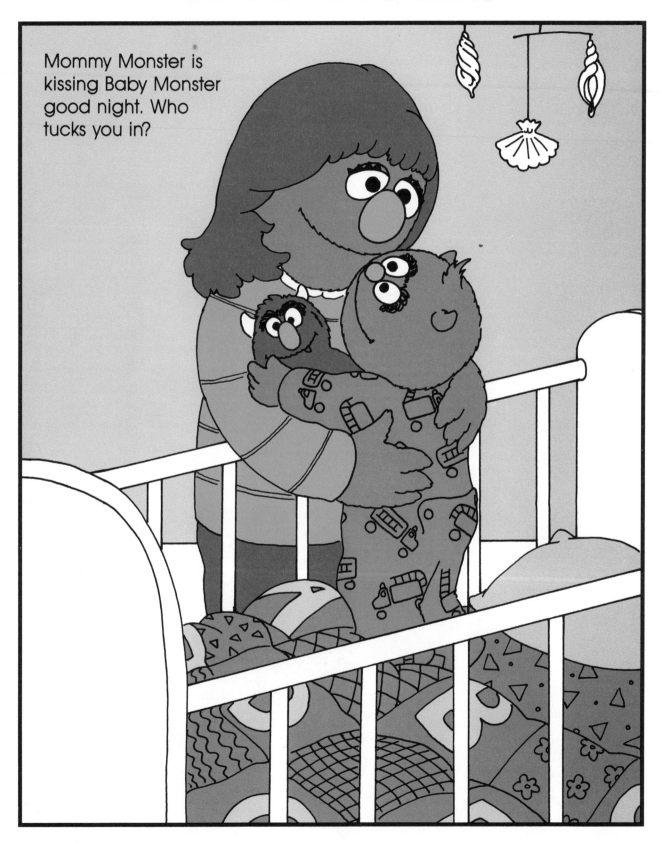

Mommy Monster is kissing Baby Monster good night. Who tucks you in?